Olivia's Secret Scribbles

Splash!

Thanks to Charlotte Costigan for her super amazing idea for this story!—M.C.

For Bridget, Rachel, Andrea, Nicole and Claudia.—D.M.

Scholastic Australia
An imprint of Scholastic Australia Pty Limited
PO Box 579 Gosford NSW 2250
ABN 11 000 614 577
www.scholastic.com.au

Part of the Scholastic Group
Sydney • Auckland • New York • Toronto • London • Mexico City
• New Delhi • Hong Kong • Buenos Aires • Puerto Rico

Published by Scholastic Australia in 2022.

A catalogue record for this book is available from the National Library of Australia

ISBN: 978-1-76112-310-8

Typeset in KG First Time in Forever, Berrylicious and Sweet Lollipop.

Printed by Hang Tai Printing Company Limited.

Scholastic Australia's policy, in association with Hang Tai, is to use papers that are renewable and made efficiently from wood grown in responsibly managed forests, so as to minimise its environmental footprint.

10 9 8 7 6 5 4 3 2 22 23 24 25 26 / 2

(This means you, Ella,
and you too, Max!!!)

Super Sunday

It's holiday time! And we're staying at a GIANT family holiday resort, called Club Tropicana!

Ella and I were both allowed to invite a friend. So of course Ella chose Zoe. And I chose Matilda. ☺

Matilda is my BFF. We do everything together, like rollerskating, and playing soccer, and swinging in the hammock in my backyard.

We are going to have the BEST time at Club Tropicana. That's because there are so many super-amazing things to do here.

Volleyball
Games room
Mini golf
Relaxing by
the pool

And I'll be able to wear my SPARKLY NEW BATHERS Nanna Kate gave me for Christmas when we go swimming in the pool.

Club Tropicana is a looooooooong way away from our house. It took ALL DAY to get here.

It's dark right now, so I haven't seen any of the super-amazing activities yet. Not even the pool. ☹

I can't wait until tomorrow!

Olivia

Holiday Monday

Matilda and I both woke up super early.

We were both busting to go for a swim in the pool. And maybe try out some of the big water slides.

Mum said we had to wait until after breakfast. ☺

But breakfast took forever! Ella and Zoe wanted to try EVERYTHING in the buffet.

And so did Dad!!

As soon as breakfast finished, Matilda and I changed into our bathers, and grabbed our hats and towels. Then we raced downstairs to meet up with everyone else.

Ella and Zoe wanted to go straight over to the water slides.

But Mum said we should all have a swim **together** first.

So we did.

Nanna Kate took Max over to the Little Kids Pool while the rest of us lined up on the edge.

I couldn't wait to see what my sparkly bathers looked like in the water. People might even think I was a **mermaid!**

We followed Mum and Dad down the steps into the shallow end of the pool.

I ♥ swimming! Our family always goes to our local pool in the summer. Sometimes I even have **races** with them. Mum always wins. ☺

We didn't do any races today though. We just swam across the pool, from one side to the other. Just like a little family of ducks.

More and more people started to arrive. They were:

swimming

and diving from the diving board

and floating around on pool toys

and doing handstands underwater.

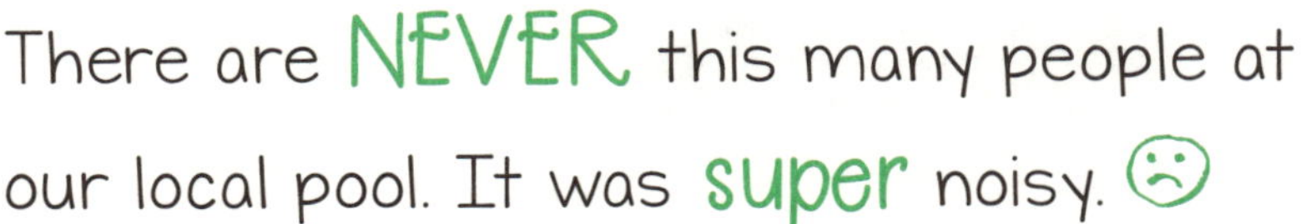

There are **NEVER** this many people at our local pool. It was **super** noisy. ☹

Ella and Zoe climbed out and raced over to the big water slides. Dad went with them.

He ♥s the Big Tornado!

Mum climbed out and stretched out on a sun lounge by the side of the pool.

After a few more minutes, Matilda and I climbed out. We ran over to the water fountain to get a drink.

Then we raced back to the side of the pool. The middle part this time.

Matilda jumped in straightaway.

But I stayed right where I was, on the side of the pool. The water looked very blue. And VERY deep.

Everyone was laughing and yelling and screaming and shouting REALLY, REALLY LOUDLY.

And I couldn't see any empty places to jump into without bumping into someone. ☹

'Come on, Olivia!' Matilda called. 'I want to show you how to swim **underwater!'**

I moved a bit closer to the edge. Then I held my breath and began counting backwards from ten. I was definitely, positively, **FOR SURE** going to jump in when I got down to one.

Ten . . .

Nine . . .

Eight . . .

Seven . . .

Six . . .

Five . . .

Four . . .

Three . . .

Water went
up my nose.

And into my ears.

And my eyes.

And my mouth.

YUK!

I was coughing so hard I couldn't stop.

There were **way** too many people in the big pool now. As well as too much shouting and splashing.

So I waved to Matilda to let her know I wasn't getting back into the pool again after all.

Then I went over to the Little Kids pool to play with Max and Nanna Kate instead.

Olivia

Water Slide Tuesday

We went out to the pool after breakfast again this morning.

This time, Mum said it was OK for Ella and Zoe to go straight over to the **big** water slides.

Matilda and I sat on the side of the pool, watching Ella and Zoe having fun.

The water slides were so **high up!** Much higher than the monkey bars at school.

And they looked **SUPER SLIPPERY** too. Much more slippery than the big slide in the park.

Matilda tapped me on the arm.

'Come on,' she said. 'Let's go for a swim instead. Last one in is a **rotten banana!**'

Then she stood up and jumped into the pool.

I **wriggled** over to the edge and looked down at the water.

I dipped one foot in.

Then the other one.

I looked around to make sure those noisy girls from yesterday weren't standing beside me. I didn't want them splashing my face again.

They weren't. So I wriggled even closer to the edge.

Matilda waved to me. **'Look!'** she called. 'It's not even that deep!'

Then she took a big breath and dived down so she could do a **handstand**.

I could see her feet sticking out of the water, like two flags.

Then she bobbed back up to the top again.

I took a big breath too. Then I started to slide my whole body into the pool, just like a slippery eel.

I waved to Matilda.

But she didn't wave back.

She was **TOO BUSY** talking to two girls.

And they looked **EXACTLY LIKE** the girls who splashed me yesterday!

Then they all took turns to see who could make water splash the furthest.

And who could do the splashiest jumps.

And heaps of other splashy stuff like that.

I didn't want Matilda's new friends to know that I was scared of the deep water in the noisy pool.

Or getting splashed again.

Or water going up my nose and into my mouth, making me cough.

So I went over to where Mum was sitting in the shade with her book, and chatted to her instead.

She even ordered us some fancy drinks!

I can always go swimming with Matilda tomorrow.

☺livia

After dinner

We all had dinner in the hotel café tonight.

And **guess** who came over to our table?

Matilda's new friends from the pool!

Charlotte and Grace asked Matilda if she wanted to play mini golf with them and their dad tomorrow.

'Would that be OK?' Matilda asked Mum and Dad.

They smiled and nodded. 'Sure,' said Dad. 'I might even pop along too.'

'Can I bring my friend Olivia?' Matilda asked Charlotte and Grace. Then she smiled at me. 'We do *everything* together, don't we?'

'Yep,' I said, smiling back. Mini golf sounded like HEAPS of fun. And I wouldn't need to worry about getting splashed or noisy people doing water bombs on a golf course. ☺

I crossed my fingers under the table.

'Ple–e–ease say yes,' I thought.

YAY! It's going to be great!

Olivia

Wonderful Wednesday

Matilda and I played mini golf with Charlotte and Grace this morning.

Their dad played too. My dad wore a SUPER daggy outfit. It was sooo embarrassing.

First we chose our balls and putters. Everyone had to pick a different colour.

Mine were yellow, like the sunshine. And Matilda's were blue. Just like the water in the pool.

Then we played a game of Eeny Meeny Miny Moe, to see who would get to go first.

I crossed my fingers tight, hoping it would be me. I love playing games like mini golf. And I wanted everyone to see that I was good at *something*.

But Charlotte won. So she went first. She put her pink ball down on the ground and took a big swing with her putter.

Her ball went shooting off to the side,

then rolled under a windmill.

It took her FOUR more goes to putt it into the hole.

Matilda went next. But her putts were too soft. It took her SIX goes to get it in.

Finally, it was my turn. And guess where my ball ended up?

Smack bang in the middle of a big pond.

OOPS! Not MORE water!

It wasn't very deep though. Not like the big pool.

PHEW! ☺

Dad helped me to scoop out the ball with a big scooper.

Then I put my ball back on the ground so I could have another go.

I hit my ball again. SUPER hard.

This time it went all the way up to the hole!

It spun around

and around

and around

the top

until finally . . .

It dropped inside.

I ♥ mini golf. It's the BEST game in the whole world!

Olivia

A bit later

Everyone was feeling **hot** and **sticky** after our game. So, as soon as we got back to our rooms we all changed into our bathers.

Then we raced outside to the pool.

Ella and Zoe were back on the **big** water slides again. They'd made some new friends, too.

And Nanna Kate and Max were back in the Little Kids Pool.

Charlotte and Grace jumped in straightaway.

Matilda held out her hand towards me.

'Come on,' she said. 'We can jump in together too.'

But I shook my head, even though I was **BUSTING** to get in the pool. The water looked so cool.

'Maybe I'll come in a bit later,' I told her.

'Aren't you hot?' Matilda asked. 'I'm BOILING!'

I shook my head. Everything was **too splashy** again.

'We don't have to jump in if you don't want to,' Matilda added. 'We can go down the stairs like we did with your mum and dad.'

I nearly said yes. Matilda is my BFF. She was trying **SO** hard to get me to come into the pool with her, and I didn't want to let her down.

But then *another* kid did a big water bomb, right in front of me:

and I changed my mind.

I didn't want to tell Matilda I was scared of the splashy water. So I told a little fib instead. 'I need to tell Mum something,' I said.

'OK,' sighed Matilda. 'See you soon.'

She swam over to where Charlotte and Grace were throwing a stripy beach ball around, and joined in the fun.

I wanted to play beach ball catchy too. I **REALLY** did. But there were too many other noisy kids in the pool.

They might crash into me.

Or into each other.

Or splash water in my eyes or up my nose.

Again!

I waved both my arms in the air and called out Matilda's name. Really, REALLY loudly.

The beach ball flew towards me. Matilda stopped playing **beach ball catchy** and looked up at me.

She swam over to the edge of the pool and I leaned down and gave the ball back to her.

'Are you coming in now?' she asked. **'Yay!'**

I shook my head.

'I've had a **really cool idea**,' I said. 'Let's play mini golf again! I can ask Dad to take us.'

Matilda looked over at Charlotte and Grace, throwing the big beach ball to each other.

Then she looked back at me.

Matilda swam to the middle of the pool, just in time to catch the ball.

I sat down on a big sun lounger, and watched them playing.

And guess who saw me sitting there, all by myself?

Ella.

'Hi, sis,' Ella said. 'Where's Matilda?'

I pointed to the pool. 'Playing with her friends,' I said.

'Is everything OK?' Ella asked me.

I gave her a big brave smile. 'Yep,' I told her.

But inside, I didn't feel brave at all. I felt just like a big scaredy cat, too afraid to jump into the water with her friends.

'Come and play with Zoe and me,' Ella said. 'There's a really awesome water slide we haven't tried yet. It's called the Slippery Dip!'

So I did. And the Slippery Dip was heaps fun! It wasn't too high or scary like some of the other big slides.

I can't **wait** to go on it again tomorrow!

☺

☺livia

Theme Park Thursday

When I woke up this morning there was a pretty white flower on the table next to my bed.

And also, this note.

Hi Olivia,
I'm **SORRY** I didn't
play mini Golf with
you yesterday. ☹

Your **BFF**

Matilda ♡

I jumped out of bed and gave Matilda a
big hug.

We got dressed and raced each other down the stairs to the breakfast room. Everyone else in my family was already there.

And guess who was sitting next to Dad?

Charlotte and Grace's dad! He was telling him all about this super amazing mini golf course that was near our resort. It had water fountains. And sprinklers to keep you cool while you were playing. It even had a Slippery Dip, just like the one at our resort!

And guess what Dad said?

YES! ☺☺☺

So we did. Charlotte and Grace and their dad came, too.

And we all had the **BEST** time!

We played mini golf

and got **splashed** by the water fountains

and **squirted** each other with super soakers

and went on the Slippery Dip at the end of the course!

But the **best** part was the bumper boats! They were kind of like the bumper cars they have at Fun World. Except you steered them around and around a pool instead of an electric rink.

Matilda and I crashed our Bumper Boat into Dad's boat three times! ☺

It was the BEST DAY EVER!

☺livia

Today was our last day at Club Tropicana.

After breakfast, Ella and Zoe asked me if Matilda and I wanted to have a go under the Big Bucket with them.

The Big Bucket is MUCH bigger and splashier than the splashy water fountains Matilda and I jumped around under yesterday.

Plus, we'd already arranged to meet Charlotte and Grace at the pool. So I told them 'maybe later,' then raced upstairs with Matilda to get changed.

Charlotte and Grace were already in the water when we arrived at the pool.

'You go,' I said to Matilda. 'I'll just be a minute.'

'OK,' said Matilda. 'See you soon.' Then she jumped in and swam over to join our friends.

I sat on the edge, dangling my feet in the **cool blue** water.

I waved to Max and Nanna Kate, on their way to the Little Kids pool.

Then I looked over at the water slides, where Ella and Zoe were dancing around under the Big Bucket.

'Olivia! Hey!'

Someone was calling my name.

I looked down. It was Charlotte and Matilda.

Charlotte: We're going to have a floatie race. Do you want to play too?

Me: Umm . . . maybe.

Matilda: Come on. It's going to be HEAPS of fun.

Me: But I don't have any noodles.

Matilda: Either do I. Grace is going to lend me one of their floaties.

Grace: We've got two. A llama and a unicorn. But I reckon pool noodles make you go faster. ☺

Me: Ummm . . .

Then I remembered all the times I'd swum with pool noodles and floaties in our local pool. It was fun! It made me feel like a big chubby penguin, floating on top of the water.

Maybe I could borrow Max's dinosaur floatie! It would be PERFECT for a floatie race.

Me (again): Sure! I'm in. When do we start?

Charlotte and Grace: Right now!

Matilda: YAY!

Grace and Matilda ran off to get their floaties.

And I ran over to the Little Kids pool to borrow Max's.

He was having **lots** of fun splashing around with his new friends.

I ran back to the pool with Max's floatie. Then I stood on the edge, looking down at the water.

Matilda waved to me.

So I did. ☺

One.

Two.

THREE!

I was IN THE WATER!!!

And my

new sparkly

bathers looked

AMAZING!

We all lined up at the side of the pool with our floaties.

Charlotte and Grace's dad started the race.

And we were off! Kicking and floating and swimming and laughing—all the way across to the other side!

Matilda was right. It was **heaps** of fun!

Even if I did come last.

And guess what we all did after that!

KER-SPLAAAAAASSSHHHHHH!

Olivia